Up the Wooden Hill

Bedtime Stories for Little Ones

by

Bob Trotter

Illustrated by Barrie Edgar

Strategic Book Group

Strategic Book Group
P.O. Box 333
Durham CT 06422
www.StrategicBookClub.com

ISBN: 978-1-60976-139-4

Printed in the United States of America

For Bradley, Jack, Christian,
Eva and Thomas.
From Granda.

Table of Contents

Norman's Bad Day

It was a hot, sultry morning in the Serengeti Parklands of Tanzania, and perched high in an Acacia tree gazing out over the parched grass sat three vultures, Stan, Harry, and Norman.

"See anything yet?" asked Stan.

"Nope, not a thing," answered Harry. "What about you, Norm?"

"Nothing yet," answered Norman wearily.

"What's keeping everyone this morning? Don't they know it's breakfast time?" said Stan, getting very impatient.

"Maybe no one's hungry yet," replied Harry, "Or maybe they're having a lie in."

"They mightn't be hungry but I'm famished," said Stan, rubbing his tummy which had started to rumble. "No sign of any hyenas yet either I suppose."

"Nope, not a blessed soul to be seen," answered Harry, holding his wing up to his eyes, "So wotcha wanna do in the meantime?" he continued, jumping up and down on a branch.

"We could do a bit of circling overhead," replied Stan. "There's nothing like a bit of circling overhead to work up an appetite."

"Not more circling overhead," sighed Norman. "I'm sick and tired of circling overhead. Every day all we ever do is circle overhead."

"What's wrong with circling overhead?" asked Harry. "We always circle overhead. Isn't that right Stan?"

"Correct, Harry my boy, correct. We are vultures, and what vultures do best is circle overhead. I circle overhead, my father circled overhead, and my grandfather was said to be the best on the plains for circling overhead."

"So he was, Stan. My father spoke about him all the time. Said he was the best at circling overhead he had ever seen," said Harry.

"Why thank you Harry. Your dad wasn't too bad either at circling overhead . . ."

"Oh for Pete's sake, enough already with the circling overhead," interrupted Norman covering his ears with his wings. Stan and Harry both looked at one another.

"What's his problem?" asked Harry.

"Beats me," replied Stan, shrugging his shoulders. "Maybe he got out on the wrong side of the tree this morning."

"Hey Norm, what's up bro?" asked Harry.

Norman looked at his two friends and mumbled quietly, "Maybe I'm just a bit fed up with being a vulture."

"What did he say?" asked Stan, looking at Harry.

"Dunno, couldn't make out a word of it. Speak up Norm, what did you say?"

"I AM SICK AND TIRED OF BEING A VULTURE THAT'S ALL!" Norman shouted. Harry and Stan both gasped in astonishment.

"I don't believe what I just heard," said Stan. "Help me Harry, I think I'm going to faint," he continued, holding onto the tree trunk.

"He doesn't mean it," said Harry, wafting Stan with his wing. "He must be suffering from heatstroke or something."

"I *do* mean it," said Norman. "Sometimes I wish that I had been born an eagle, or a flamingo or something, anything other than an ugly vulture."

"But why?" asked Stan, trying to hold back the tears.

"Because nobody likes us Stan, that's why. When was the last time you ever heard anyone say, 'Ah look at the beautiful vulture.' Never, and do you know why? Because we're ugly, that's why. All we ever do is circle overhead, swoop down, and stick our heads into dead animals. The lions don't like us. The hyenas don't like us; even the tourists don't like us. And I for one am sick of it."

"Hyenas don't like anybody," said Harry, ruffling his feathers.

"That's not the point, Harry," said Norman.

"And as for being ugly," chuckled Stan, "when was the last time you saw Harry's wee sister. She's far from ugly, believe me."

"Yes well, she's not bad I must admit," said Norman. "But look at us three. We have big hooked beaks; big, baldy heads; long, skinny necks; and dull, black feathers. I mean, why couldn't we be bright blue, or a nice shade of pink or something? The only time we have any colour, is when we're eating. And that's another thing. Nobody has any table manners. There's always fighting and squabbling to see who can get the best bits, and none of it tastes very nice anyway. Why can't we have a nice bit of fruit, or berries, or even some nuts for a change?"

Stan and Harry both stared at Norman with their beaks wide open, not quite believing what they were hearing. "He has definitely lost his marbles," said Harry.

"He must have a fever or something," said Stan, "I mean, who ever heard of a bright blue vulture that ate nuts?"

"I don't have a fever, and I haven't lost my marbles. I just wish I was something other than a vulture that's all," said Norman quietly.

"I've just thought of something," said Harry. "If there were no vultures, then who would clean up all the dead animals from the plains, eh! Tell me that Mister I'm-too-good-to-be-a-vulture?"

"I don't know. The beetles and stuff maybe."

"Beetles and stuff!" retorted Stan getting very cross. "Come on Harry, you and me will do a bit of circling. I've heard enough of this nonsense."

"Me too," replied Harry, "Let's see who can circle the highest, and leave old misery guts to himself."

"You know something, Norm," said Stan, "we mightn't be the most beautiful looking creatures on the planet, but we all serve a purpose. You mightn't like being a vulture, but I'm afraid you're stuck with it, and there's not a thing you can do to change it." And with that, Stan and Harry spread their wings, and took off into the clear blue African sky, riding the thermals of hot air that took them higher and higher.

"We'll soon see about that," said Norman, watching them go.

Norman sat for a while wondering what to do. He looked down at his dull, black feathers and sighed. "What I need is a splash of colour," he said, looking around. Norman suddenly smiled. "Aha! The very thing. Why didn't I think of it before?" He flapped down from the tree and landed on the grass. Not too far away were a clump of bushes that were covered in brightly coloured flowers. Norman waddled over and began to pluck some of the flowers, being careful not to scratch himself on the thorns. "These will do nicely," he said as he pushed yellow, blue, and pink flowers in-between his feathers. When he was finished, he looked down at his brightly decorated feathers and chuckled to himself, "Beautiful. Now no one will even know I'm a vulture."

After making sure that the flowers were all firmly in place, Norman took off in search of some breakfast. "Now let's see if I can find something sweet and juicy for a change." After a short while, he noticed a troop of baboons enjoying some fruit that had fallen from a large papaya tree. Norman landed a short distance away, and made his way over to where some of the fruit was lying in the long grass. A very large male baboon spied him and came running towards him.

"Oy!" shrieked the baboon. "What do you want?"

"Oh nothing," replied Norman, "just to sample the delights of this beautiful looking fruit."

The baboon raised an eyebrow and looked at him very suspiciously. "When did vultures start eating fruit? You usually have your head stuck in a dead zebra or something."

"Ah, but I'm not a vulture," replied Norman stretching out his wings to show off the flowers. "See. When did you ever see a vulture with such fine, colourful feathers?"

"So what kind of bird are you then?" asked the baboon, eyeing Norman up and down, and folding his arms.

"I'm a, well yes exactly. I'm a, emm, err, bushel bird. Yes, a bushel bird. Just arrived here from the bushes high up in the mountains, don't you know?"

"Never heard of you," replied the baboon, "You look more like an ugly vulture with stupid flowers stuck in you feathers."

"No, no. I'm a bushel bird okay, and I love fruit. So if you don't mind."

"Be my guest," laughed the baboon. "In fact, let me help you." And he hurled a large papaya, which hit Norman on the beak and splattered over the front of his feathers. When all the other baboons saw what was happening, they started throwing fruit as well, some of which had rotted and smelled rather stinky. "Bushel bird indeed, you must think I'm stupid," shouted the male baboon, throwing more and more fruit. "Clear off, we don't want your kind around here."

"Yes, clear off!" shouted the rest of the baboons. Even the little ones were laughing and shouting "Baldy, baldy," as they chased Norman through the grass, hurling more rotten fruit and elephant poo after him.

Norman ran as fast as he could and took off into the sky, which was quite difficult as his wings were covered in sticky fruit juice. After a few minutes, he landed on a rocky outcrop and began to clean the fleshy bits of papaya out of his feathers. "Well that could have gone better," he said to himself. "Maybe I should try some nuts instead." Norman flew around until he saw a large tree laden with brown nuts. He landed on a thick branch, pulled off a large nut and tossed it into the air to catch in his beak.

"Oy! You! Stop!" shouted a voice above him. Norman looked up, completely forgetting about the nut that he had tossed into the air, which came back down and hit him on the top of his head. "What do you think you are doing?" said the voice. Norman peered through the leaves and there sitting on one of the very top branches was a little yellow parakeet with a huge beak.

"Did you say something?" asked Norman.

"You can't eat nuts like that," said the parakeet. "You need to take the shell off first."

"What's a shell?" asked Norman, rolling one of the nuts around in his wing.

"The hard bit on the outside," replied the parakeet. "You need to take that off so that you can get at the nut in the middle."

"I thought you just ate the whole thing," said Norman.

"Goodness me no, do you want to choke?"asked the parakeet, landing beside Norman, "Here let me show you." The little parakeet pulled off a nut and cracked it in his beak until the shell fell off and he was left with only the bit in the middle. "See, that's how you do it. Now you have a go." Norman copied what the parrot had done, and cracked the nut as hard as he could in his beak.

"Ow! Ow! I have cracked my beak instead of the nut!" shouted Norman.

"Oh dear," said the parakeet, holding his wing up to his beak and trying hard not to laugh. "Maybe vultures aren't supposed to eat nuts after all."

"It hurts! It really hurts!" yelled Norman in pain. "Do something."

"What do you want me to do?" asked the parakeet tucking into another nut. "Your beak obviously isn't made for cracking nuts. Maybe you should just stick to the things you can eat."

"Thanks a bunch," said Norman crossly. "You're a great help."

"It's not my fault," replied the parakeet. "And if you're gonna be huffy about it, you can sort your own beak out. Bye."

Norman flapped down out of the tree and sat on the grass holding his wing up to his beak, and feeling very sorry for himself. "This is just great," he sighed. "My feathers are covered in sticky fruit juice. My flowers have lost nearly all their petals, my beak throbs, and I still haven't had any breakfast." A short distance away he noticed a small tree with bright green berries. *Surely those are okay to eat,* he thought.

He waddled over to the bush and began to pick off some of the berries, being extra careful not to make his beak any sorer than it already was. When he had a large mouthful, he began to chew, very carefully. "Hmm, these don't taste too bad," he said. "In fact, they're quite nice." Norman began to feast on the berries, stuffing as many into his beak as he could. "These are lovely," he said "Soft and juicy and very sweet. Wait 'til I tell Harry and Stan about these."

Norman then heard a squeaky little voice coming from the grass at his feet.

"Excuse me," said the voice, "you haven't eaten any of those, have you?"

Norman looked down, and there at his feet was a little brown coloured mouse.

"Why?"asked Norman. "What's wrong with them. They taste lovely."

"Dear me," said the mouse, "how can I put this delicately. They make you, emm, go."

"What do you mean?" asked Norman.

"Just what I said. All the animals eat them if they are having problems going," answered the mouse. "And even then, they would only eat a couple. How many have you eaten?"

"Five or six...mouthfuls," Norman replied.

"Then you will have absolutely no problem going," laughed the mouse.

Norman looked totally confused. "Going where?" He then heard an urgling and a gurgling noise in his belly, followed by a rumbling, and then a splishing and a sploshing, and it felt as if his insides were doing somersaults. "Uh oh! I think I need to go!" exclaimed Norman as his belly turned over and over.

"That's what I'm talking about," said the mouse. "You should never eat those berries unless you need help and are feeling a bit bunged up, if you see what I mean."

"Sorry, can't stop," cried Norman, trying to take off with one wing, and hold his bottom with the other.

Eventually, after having to land in the long grass quite a few times, Norman made it home. His feathers were matted and sticky, his beak was really sore, his belly was still feeling a bit iffy, and he had been to the loo more times in one day than he had for a month. "I am never, ever, going to complain about being a vulture again," he said as he lay down totally exhausted and fell fast asleep, even though it was nowhere near bedtime.

The next morning, Harry and Stan were perched as usual in their favourite Acacia tree.

"See anything yet?" asked Stan.

"Nope, nothing yet," answered Harry.

"This is ridiculous," complained Stan. "I'm fed up having to sit here every morning waiting for someone to kill something so that we can have breakfast."

"Well, there's no point in moaning about it," replied Harry, "unless you want to try fruit and nuts like Norman."

"No thanks. Speaking of Norman, I wonder how he got on yesterday," said Stan.

"Dunno, haven't seen him since. So what do you want to do in the meantime?" Stan was about to answer, when Norman landed on the branch beside him.

"We could do a bit of circling overhead," he said.

Harry and Stan both smiled. "The very thing," said Stan. "There's nothing like a bit of circling overhead to work up an appetite. Gave up on berries and the like have you?"

"Definitely. As you say Stan, we mightn't be the most beautiful looking birds in the world, but we serve a purpose."

"Exactly," said Harry, "We all serve a purpose. And by the way, I betcha I can circle the highest."

And with that, the three friends took off circling higher and higher until they were only small black specks in the cloudless, Tanzanian sky.

The End

Sidney's Sore Throat

Sidney the giraffe had a problem, because Sidney had a very, very sore throat that was making him feel thoroughly miserable.

"Whatever is wrong with you today, Sidney?" asked Doris, one of the older giraffes. "You are moping about like a warthog with a sore tusk."

"I have a very sore throat," croaked Sidney. "I can't eat or drink anything."

"Oh my," replied Doris. "That is a problem. A giraffe with a sore throat is as bad as an elephant with a runny nose. You must get it seen to, sweetie."

"I have tried everything I can think of," replied Sidney. "I haven't eaten all morning and I have been gargling with salt water but nothing seems to work— stupid sore throat."

Thelma and Sheldon arrived. "What's all the kerfuffle about?" asked Sheldon.

"It's Sidney, dearest. He has a very sore throat and I was just telling him that he would need to get it seen to," replied Doris.

"Oh indeed, indeed," said Thelma, "We can't have a giraffe with a sore throat; that's as bad as an elephant with—"

"Yes, I know, a runny nose," interrupted Sidney rather rudely.

"You need to see Mbeki," said Sheldon.

"Who?" enquired Sidney.

"The local doctor from the village, dearest," said Doris. "He holds a clinic in his hut every morning to help animals who are feeling a tad under the weather."

"Oh yes!" exclaimed Thelma excitedly. "I completely forgot about him. Lovely man he is, always willing to help. Very well spoken and mannerly, for a human. You really should go and see him sweetheart."

Doris, Thelma, and Sheldon left Sidney and loped off towards some very succulent looking young trees. "Nice boy, Sidney," Thelma said to the others, "but he can be a bit scatterbrained at times."

"Oh I know, I know," replied Doris, "very like his mother. She was a bit scatty as well, poor soul. Fell in love with a crocodile once, but it all ended in tears."

"Yes, crocodile tears," giggled Sheldon.

Doris and Thelma laughed. "Really, Sheldon," said Doris, "you are quite awful at times."

Sidney was fed up. He didn't want to go to the doctor and was very nervous. He had never been to a doctor before. But it was either that or starve. So in the end, he decided he had no choice; the doctor it was. He had never even been to the village before, and wasn't exactly too sure where it was, so reluctantly he headed off along a road by the side of the river. *I'm sure I will find someone that can help*, he thought to himself.

As he walked along the path, he soon met a large, grumpy-looking water buffalo that was chewing grass by the side of the track. "Excuse me," said Sidney in his politest, least croaky voice possible. "Beautiful morning isn't it? I was wondering if you could possibly tell me the way to the village."

"What?" replied the buffalo crossly. "Can't you see I'm having breakfast."

"Yes, I'm so sorry for disturbing you while you're

eating," replied Sidney, "but I am trying to get to Dr. Mbeki, and I was wondering if this is the way."

"Mbeki!" said the buffalo getting even more cross. "Never heard of the chap. Now clear off and let me have my breakfast in peace."

"Yes, of course. Sorry," said Sidney, walking off rather quickly.

"The cheek if it!" he heard the buffalo mumble. "Young upstart, disturbing a chap's breakfast to ask about an Mbeki. Hah! No respect for their elders nowadays these young animals."

Sidney left the buffalo still going on about how in his day young animals weren't allowed to speak to their elders, unless they were spoken to first, and certainly never during breakfast.

What a grouch, thought Sidney as he walked on.

Further down the road Sidney saw a little deer hiding in the undergrowth. "Hello there," he said. "I wonder if you could help me." But before he could ask anymore, the deer screeched in a very startled, high-pitched voice before running off deeper into the woods. *How very strange*, thought Sidney, as he watched the little deer disappear further into the forest.

Sidney then heard laughing above him, and saw some young Colobus monkeys playing high up in the trees. "I think you scared her off, Lofty," said one.

"Yes well, I didn't mean to," replied Sidney. "I was only going to ask if she knew the way to the village, that's all."

"We know the way to the village," said another, "but we're not telling you."

"Why ever not?" asked Sidney.

"Cos our mum is always telling us not to speak to any strange animals," replied the young monkey, "and she says that with your long neck, and your horns on top of your head, you're the strangest looking one of the lot."

All the monkeys laughed at Sidney and began making faces, blowing raspberries, and throwing rotten fruit at him. Sidney felt very embarrassed. "It's just as well you're up that tree!" he shouted.

"Yeah, or what?" said one of the monkeys sticking his tongue out.

"Or I would give you a clip around the ear," said Sidney crossly.

"Oh yeah, you and whose army?" yelled the monkey laughing even more.

Sidney decided it was probably best to ignore the young monkeys and move on. "Cheeky twerps!" he shouted back at them as he walked off.

The Colobus monkeys were now laughing so much; they were rolling about the grass on their backs shouting, "Lofty, lofty!" at him as he continued on down the road, trying his best to retain as much of his dignity as possible.

He hadn't gone very far when he heard a voice squawk above him, "If you are looking for the village, it's about a mile down the road. In fact, I can see it from up here."

Sidney looked up squinting through the leaves, and there perched on a branch in a very high tree was a little red, green, and blue parrot. "Thank you very much," replied Sidney.

"Is it Dr. Mbeki you are going to see?" asked the parrot.

"Yes. Do you know him?" answered Sidney.

"Not very well," said the parrot. "I had to go to him once when I chipped my beak on a walnut. Sore it was, but he sorted it out and in a few days I was as right as rain. What's up with you then?"

"Sore throat," replied Sidney.

"Oh dear," said the parrot. "Nasty things, sore throats, especially if you're a giraffe. Anyway, just go around the next couple of bends and you're there. See ya!"

"Thank you!" shouted Sidney as the parrot flew off. "What a nice parrot," Sidney said to himself, "and so helpful."

Soon, Sidney was at the village. He was looking around wondering where he had to go when he saw a very large, very round lady in a brightly coloured dress and headscarf marching quite purposefully towards him.

"Are you here to see the doctor?" she asked.

"Err, yes," replied Sidney nervously.

"Good. Follow me," said the round lady, and she headed off towards a large hut at the side of the village. Sidney followed. "Giraffes round the back and then take a seat in the waiting room," she continued.

Sidney went in, sat down on a large seat, and crossed his legs. Inside were two other patients waiting to see the doctor. There was a crocodile with toothache, who was reading a very old copy of *Waterhole Weekly* with the headline, "Wildebeest. We've had enough." And sitting as far away from the crocodile as possible was a white zebra that was shaking uncontrollably, and who appeared to have lost his black stripes. *Well I never*, thought Sidney, *I always thought zebras were black with white stripes*. On the opposite wall there was a very large notice which read.

ATTENTION!

UNDER NO CIRCUMSTANCES ARE ANY ANIMALS WAITING TO SEE THE DOCTOR ALLOWED TO EAT ANY OTHER ANIMALS.

BY ORDER

Dr. Mbeki.

"Thank goodness for that," said Sidney. The large, round lady then appeared.

"Name?" she asked.

"Sidney," replied Sidney.

"And what is the problem, Sidney?"

"Sore throat," he replied, pointing to his throat.

"Okay, very well," said the round lady. "I will let the doctor know and he will see you shortly."

The zebra was then called and disappeared through

a door at the back of the hut, jibbering and shaking as he went.

The crocodile nodded at Sidney. "That's where the doc is," he said. "Old Jeremy there, had a close encounter with a lioness and turned completely white. But I dare say a few pills and a splash of black paint will sort him out."

"Really," answered Sidney, "What about you? Have you been here before then?"

"Me, lots of times. I have weak teeth apparently. Keep breaking them on wildebeest and the like." Sidney was hoping that the crocodile had seen the notice on the wall.

"So why are you here?" continued the crocodile.

"Sore throat," answered Sidney.

"Ahh," replied the crocodile. "I get that sometimes when a bone gets stuck. Maybe that's what is wrong with you."

"No, I don't think so," replied Sidney, trying his

best not to look nervous. "I don't eat anything with bones in it."

"That's right," replied the crocodile, "I forgot you giraffes are all veggies. Me, I could never be a veggie, not that there's anything wrong with it mind you, each to his own I say. But I love my meat too much," and he grinned, showing row upon row of very sharp teeth.

The large, round lady then came back. "Okay Marvin," she said, "the doctor will see you now." Marvin got up and followed her after setting down the magazine he was reading.

"Hope your throat gets better soon," he said, winking at Sidney. "And who knows, maybe I will see you down at the water hole some day."

"Err, yes, that would be nice," said Sidney, "NOT," he continued under his breath when Marvin had left.

Sidney rubbed his throat as he waited, hoping that it would suddenly and miraculously be better. He even tried swallowing a few times, but his poor throat was still as sore as ever. A short time later, the large, round lady came back and waved at him to follow her.

He was led into a back room which was full of all sorts of bits and bobs and bottles of stuff, which made it smell very peculiar. Dr. Mbeki then came in. He was a short stocky little man with red hair and eyes that appeared to be too big for his face, and he was wearing a long white coat, which had a stethoscope hanging out of the pocket. "Sit, Sidney, sit," he said in a very jolly voice. "Haven't had a giraffe in here for ages. Now, nurse tells me you have a very sore throat."

"Yes," replied Sidney hoarsely, "I can't swallow anything."

"Well, we can't be having that," replied Dr. Mbeki, "So let's take a look and see what the problem is."

He disappeared out of the room and came back with a pair of step ladders and a torch. "Now open your mouth as wide as you can," said Dr. Mbeki, climbing the ladder, "and say aaaaah." Sidney did as he was told, while Dr. Mbeki shone the torch down his throat. "Ahah!" exclaimed Dr. Mbeki so loudly it made Sidney jump. "I see now what the problem is. Nurse, fetch me the extra long, giraffe-sized tweezers please."

Very carefully, Dr. Mbeki put the extra long, giraffe-sized tweezers down Sidney's throat, and pulled out a large thorn, which he showed to Sidney.

Immediately, Sidney's throat felt a lot better. "See Sidney," said Dr. Mbeki, "this is what happens when you don't chew your food properly; it gets stuck." Sidney blushed and was given a glass of pineapple and mint juice to soothe his throat. "Just eat berries for the rest of the day, and by tomorrow you should be fine," said Dr. Mbeki, climbing down the ladder. "And remember; always chew your food properly."

"I will. Thank you very much, Doctor," replied Sidney, feeling slightly embarrassed.

"Not at all, you're welcome," replied Dr Mbeki dropping the thorn in a waste bin. "And pop in again if you're passing. Even just for a chat". Sidney thanked the doctor again and headed out the door.

Do you know what? he thought to himself, *Thelma was right. Dr. Mbeki is a very nice man, for a human, and that didn't hurt one little bit. Now, I wonder where Marvin has gone, as I have had quite enough excitement for one day.* Sidney suddenly stopped and looked around, deciding which way to go. "Oh dear, which is the way home?" he said. "Well, I know one thing," he laughed as he headed away from the village, "if I get lost, I certainly will NOT be asking any water buffalo."

The End

The Dinosaur That Was Afraid to Fly

Long, long ago, before there were shops or ice cream, before wine gums, Game Boys, Nintendo's, or mobile phones, and even before people, there were dinosaurs, all kinds of dinosaurs. Some were as big as houses and some were as small as mice. Some were ferocious, and some were gentle. Some hunted other dinosaurs, and some were happy just to eat shrubs and plants. Most lived on the land, roaming across the great valleys and forests, and some flew through the air, catching fish from the streams and lakes. All that is except one, and his name was Brian.

Brian was a pterodactyl—a sort of flying dinosaur—with great wings for gliding and a long beak that was just right for scooping fish out of the water. There was, however, one problem; Brian was scared of flying. Every day his dad would take him to the edge of the cliff where he lived, and every day they would walk back home because Brian was too frightened to jump.

"Well, how did it go today, any luck?" said his mum when they arrived home.

"No, same as usual," answered his dad crossly. "He gets up to the edge, looks down, and says he feels dizzy."

"Well, it *is* a long way down, dear," answered his mum.

"That's not the point, Muriel," said his dad. "He's a skyglider for heaven's sake. He is supposed to jump off high cliffs and glide around the sky, shouting at the landwalkers. That's what makes us better than them."

"Never mind," said his mum gently. "Maybe tomorrow."

"Tomorrow!" exclaimed his dad. "That, my dear, is about as likely as old Brutus the tyrannosaur becoming a vegetarian. Anyway," he sighed, "I said I would meet Stan and catch something for tea. You see if you can talk some sense into him," and off he flew feeling very embarrassed that HIS son was the only one on the cliff that hadn't flown yet, and afraid that they were fast becoming a laughing stock.

Brian looked at his mum with tears in his eyes. "Dad's cross, isn't he?" he asked.

"Not so much cross as disappointed, dear," replied his mum. "When I first met your dad he was a great flier, the best on the cliff. He would glide across the lake laughing at the landwalkers, and then he would loop the loop and land back on the ledge. Very dashing he was, and I suppose he wants you to be the same."

"I do want to fly," said Brian, "it's just that when I stand at the edge and look down, the landwalkers look so tiny that I get really scared."

"Well," said his mum, "if you want to fly, that is something that you are going to have to overcome."

"I know," said Brian. "I will try again tomorrow Mum, I promise."

"That's a good boy," said his mum. "Now off you go and wash your wings before your tea."

Brian waddled off down to the stream that cascaded over the cliff as a large waterfall. As he washed his wings in the cold water, the sky above him was filled with young pterodactyls laughing as they dive-bombed the landwalkers. That was their favourite game, and as Brian watched, he wished that he could join in. "One day," he said looking at the others, "I will fly. I will be the best on the cliff and do more loops than anyone else, and Dad will be really proud of me." Then he slowly walked back home to where his dad had returned with their tea.

The next day, Brian and his dad walked up to the cliff edge as usual. "Well," said his dad, "do you think we could try today?" Brian looked down. The lake below seemed no bigger than a large puddle and all the landwalkers looked like tiny dots, drinking or washing. Brian gulped. He was concentrating so hard on the lake below that he didn't notice his dad behind him, and the next thing he knew he was falling through the air.

"Stretch out your wings!" his dad shouted. But Brian was too terrified.

"I can't!" he screamed, "Daaaaaaaad help meeeeeeee!"

"Oh for Pete's sake," said his dad, jumping off the cliff to catch Brian before he hit the water.

All around the lake the landwalkers heard the commotion and looked up. "Oh look!" said one, "A skyglider who can't glide." The landwalkers laughed.

"I wonder who it is?" said another. Then they saw Terence catch Brian just before he splashed into the lake.

"Oy Terence!" shouted the first landwalker. "What's wrong with your boy? Forgotten his wings has he?"

"Maybe he wants to be a landwalker," shouted another.

"Or a seaswimmer," shouted someone else. All around the lake the landwalkers erupted into fits of laughter.

Brian's dad was furious. He landed back at the top of the cliff and dumped Brian into some bushes. "That's it!" he shouted at Brian, "I have never been so humiliated in all my life. Did you hear all the landwalkers laughing at us?"

"I'm sorry, Dad," replied Brian, "but I didn't think you were going to push me."

"Well, I am finished trying to teach you," continued his dad, "from now on Brian, you are on your own."

Brian's dad flew off furious, with the laughs of the landwalkers still ringing in his ears.

Brian lifted himself out of the bushes, and winced as he began pulling the thorns out of his bottom. "Maybe I should become a landwalker," he said to himself. "I am never going to be a skyglider."

"There is nothing wrong with landwalkers, dear boy," a voice behind him growled. "Landwalkers were here long before skygliders and are therefore far superior. Seaswimmers were here first, of course. But they are such stupid creatures; they are hardly worth a mention." Brian turned round and froze. It was Brutus, the tyrannosaur.

"Uh oh," said Brian, looking for somewhere to hide.

"What's wrong, little one; you aren't scared of little old me are you?" Brutus continued. "You know it has been such a long time since I had a young skyglider for dinner. But why are you not flying off? Oh! I forgot," sneered Brutus, "I saw you with your father and you're too scared to fly. Aren't you?" he laughed, opening his massive jaws and running at Brian.

Brian yelled and ran as fast as his little legs would carry him. "Dad!" he screamed, looking up at his dad as he flew off, "Help me. It's Brutus!" But his dad was too far away to hear him.

"Do you know what? I don't think he can hear you," laughed Brutus. Brian ran on through the bushes and ferns with Brutus right behind, laughing and growling.

As Brian ran for his life, his dad was telling his friend Stan about what happened earlier at the lake. "You just need to be patient," Stan was saying. "All kids are different. Fly back and have another go."

Terence sighed, "Maybe you're right. I'll go and find him and see if he wants to try again."

"That's the ticket," said Stan. "And don't push him this time."

"I won't," replied Terence. "I think he has been scared enough for one day." And off he flew.

Brian meanwhile had run right to the edge of the cliff and was trapped. "What are you going to do now?" laughed Brutus. "Jump?" Brian looked down at the lake far below, sobbing his little heart out. "Boo hoo, poor little skyglider," taunted Brutus, "Doesn't know how to glide and doesn't have his daddy here to help him."

Just then, Brian heard his dad's voice shouting above him. "Jump, Brian! You have to jump."

Brutus heard the voice as well, and looked up, "It's too late," he roared lunging at Brian.

At that very same second, however, Brian closed his eyes and jumped. Brutus was going so fast that he couldn't stop and ran past Brian over the edge of the cliff. "Spread your wings!" Terence shouted. Brian did what he was told and instead of tumbling down into the lake something marvellous happened—he began to glide.

"Look Dad!" he shouted. "I'm flying, I'm flying! I am a skyglider after all. Wheeeeeee!" he exclaimed as he began to twist and turn around the sky.

Below him there was an almighty crash as Brutus landed in the lake. A huge spray of water flew up into the air, soaking all the other landwalkers around the water's edge. "Well, I never," said one as he shook the water from himself. "What a strange day this has been. First we had a skyglider trying to be a landwalker, and now we have Brutus, a landwalker, trying to be a skyglider." Again fits of uncontrollable laughter erupted all around the lake, as Brutus climbed out onto the bank coughing and spluttering and feeling very, very silly.

Terence flew down to be with his son. "Well done, Brian," he said. "I am so proud of you. You really taught old Brutus a lesson," he laughed, putting his wing around his son.

"Thanks Dad," replied Brian. "And talking of lessons, will you teach me so that I can be as good as you?"

"Of course," said his dad, "but first, I think we better let your mum know."

And that's how it was. Terence taught Brian all he knew about flying, and every day Brian got better and better, until he was the best flier on the cliff. And as for old Brutus, well, after being outwitted by a young skyglider, he moved to another valley, as he was far too embarrassed to show his face around the lake ever again.

The End

Jefferson Goes To Town

Jefferson the leopard cub was bored. "Ho hum!" he sighed as he lay on the grass of the enclosure at the zoo where he lived, with his chin resting on his paws.

"What's wrong with you?" laughed Loki, his little sister, jumping on his back to try and catch his tail.

"I am so bored," Jefferson sighed, pushing her off. "Nothing exciting ever happens here. It's just the same old thing day in, day out. We get up, run around, play for the visitors, eat the same old food, and then go back to bed. It is SO boring."

"Well, what do you want to do?" asked Loki, tugging at an old tractor tyre.

"I don't know," replied Jefferson, shrugging his shoulders. "Something different for a change."

"Go and chase the crows and magpies, you love doing that," suggested Loki with a mouthful of rubber.

"Boring," replied Jefferson.

"Roar at the chimps and baboons then."

"Boring," replied Jefferson again.

"I know, see if you can beat your record for climbing the big tree," Loki continued.

"BORING, BORING, BORING," huffed Jefferson with a big yawn.

"Know what your problem is Jefferson?" said his sister crossly. "You don't know what you want," and sticking her tongue out, she went off to climb the big tree herself.

"I do know what I want," said Jefferson to himself, ignoring his little sister. "To get away from here and see the world outside." As Jefferson lay imagining what it would be like to be away from the zoo, his keeper Bob arrived.

"Dinner time," said Bob cheerfully.

Oh great, thought Jefferson, *more raw meat, just what I always wanted*. Bob opened the gate of the enclosure to carry in the buckets of meat, leaving it slightly ajar behind him. Jefferson lifted his head and saw his chance. As quick as lightning, he raced past Bob, out of the gate, and onto the roadway that snaked its way around the zoo.

"I'm free," laughed Jefferson as he went running and jumping towards the exit. Needless to say when the visitors to the zoo saw Jefferson, they went running and jumping towards the exit as well.

"HELP, A WILD ANIMAL HAS ESCAPED!" they yelled panic stricken as they ran towards the car park. Jefferson stopped in his tracks, and looked round feeling very worried.

A wild animal has escaped, he thought to himself. *Maybe I should follow the humans and get out of here.*

As Jefferson strutted towards the exit, there was absolute chaos. People were running in every direction shouting and screaming, tripping over buggies and prams, climbing up lampposts, dropping bags of potato chips, sandwiches, and ice cream cones. Parents were lifting their children, who were giggling and laughing onto their shoulders, while others were climbing up onto the roofs of buildings or locking themselves in their cars. The keepers were running about not knowing what to do, and poor old Bob had run so hard that his face was bright red; so he had to sit down to get to get his breath back, and mop his brow with a large, white handkerchief.

I wonder what all the commotion is about, thought Jefferson as he headed through the car park and along the road that led into town. As he trotted on, Jefferson nodded and waved occasionally at people who were jumping back into their cars, or running back into their houses and staring out of the windows. "Morning," he said to anyone he met. "Lovely morning, but I hear it might rain later," he continued in as friendly a manner as he could. But no matter who he tried to talk to they just screamed and ran away shouting for help.

Humans are such strange creatures, thought Jefferson as he walked along the side of the road, not noticing that cars were beeping their horns and screeching their brakes as the drivers tried not to crash into one another. He soon came to a park with swings, slides, roundabouts, and climbing frames. "Wow!" said Jefferson, "That looks like fun." So in he went. As he walked along the grass towards the swings and stuff, all the kids that were playing on them were quickly gathered up by their mums and dads, thrown into buggies, or grabbed by the arms and pulled and pushed towards the park gates, kicking and screaming. Jefferson watched them run away, puzzled.

"I wonder what's wrong with them," he said, sitting down on the grass watching them go. "Ah well, at least I have the whole place to myself." He climbed up the steps of the largest slide, and sat at the top. Then he gave himself a push and went flying off the end, landing with a bump on his bottom. "Wheee, that was great. I must have another go," he laughed, running back around, and climbing up the steps. "Loki doesn't know what she's missing. This is far better that climbing that stupid tree."

After he had gone on the slide about another ten times, Jefferson made his way over to the swings. *I wonder what this does*, he thought. He jumped up onto a swing, which immediately flew backwards dumping Jefferson on the ground, banging his head. "Ouch! That hurt," he said, rubbing the back of his head with his paw. Jefferson then heard shouts behind him; it was Bob with the other zoo keepers and some policemen.

"Jefferson," shouted Bob, "stay where you are. It's time to go back to the zoo."

"Uh oh, looks like I'm in trouble," said Jefferson as he bolted as fast as he could across the grass, through the trees, and out of the gates at the far end of the park. "If they want to take me back to the zoo," he said, "they are going to have to catch me first."

As he ran along the streets into the town centre, Jefferson couldn't help but notice that they were all deserted. Everywhere there were shops, offices, and cafes, but nobody seemed to be doing any shopping, or having a cup of coffee, or eating a burger, or anything. Not a living soul could be seen. *Where is everyone?* thought Jefferson, as he slowly walked along looking in the shop windows. *I always imagined the town would have loads of people in it, but it's empty.*

One of the shops he looked into was a lady's clothes shop with a display of coats in the window. On one of the dummies was a coat, which looked exactly the same as his, except that it was a fake. Jefferson studied it for a while, moving his head from side to side. *Hmm,* he thought, *why would a human want to dress like a leopard?* Then he smiled, *I wonder what I would look like dressed as a human?* Jefferson walked in through the front door, "Hello!" he called, "Anyone here?" But no one answered. All around the shop were rails and rails of coats, jumpers, blouses, hats and scarves, as well as shoes and handbags. Jefferson tried on some coats but they were all far too big, and tripped him up as he tried to walk around. He then tried to put on some shoes, but couldn't get his paws into them. So at last, he settled for a hat.

The first hat he put on was red with blue flowers around it. Jefferson looked at himself in the mirror, "Nope, not quite me." He then tried on a large, black hat with a white and yellow feather, but the feather hung down the front of his face tickling his nose, and making him sneeze. Next he tried a tiara that a lady would wear when getting married. *Nice*, thought Jefferson, *but not very practical*. Lastly, he tried a straw hat that you would wear at the beach in the summer. Jefferson smiled as he admired himself in the mirror. "Perfect," he said and walked out of the shop back onto the street.

Jefferson strolled on pausing to take a drink from a fountain in the town square, when his tummy began to rumble. "Gosh, I'm starving," he said looking round, "I wonder where I could get something to eat?" Further down the street he came to a delicatessen, which had lots of cakes, buns, and other goodies in the window. Jefferson licked his lips and walked in. Again, there was no one about, so he walked around the counter and helped himself. Jefferson purred with delight, and very soon his face and whiskers were covered in cream, jam, and chocolate as he stuffed as many buns, cakes, and biscuits into his mouth as he possibly could. When he had eaten his fill, he left and made his way towards a very large building at the far end of the town, the local leisure centre.

As soon as he walked in, Jefferson could smell the water and followed his nose until he came to the pool. Gingerly, he dipped one paw into the water and felt that it was nice and warm. He set his hat down on a chair, took a massive leap into the air, and landed with a great splash in the middle of the pool. "This is great fun!" he shouted as he rolled onto his back, shooting a fountain of water up into the air.

At the far end of the pool was a large inflatable, which the kids used for playing on. Jefferson paddled over to it and tried to climb up. Unfortunately, it was so wet and slippery that every time he tried to climb up, he just slid back down. He tried once more only this time, he flicked out his claws to get a better grip. Suddenly, there was a loud *bang, pop,* and *whoosh* as the inflatable burst, and all the air started to rush out from where his claws had tore a large hole in its side. In a few minutes, the inflatable was as flat as a pancake and floating on top of the water, useless. "Hmm, maybe I had better move on," said Jefferson, looking very guilty, and hoping that no one had seen him.

He swam over to the side of the pool and climbed out. After he had shaken himself and put his hat back on, he walked back out into the main hall of the leisure centre. "Hmmm, something smells nice," he said as he sniffed the air. Jefferson followed the smell until he came to the café where he sat down at a table.

He looked around waiting for someone to come and serve him, but nobody came. *The service in this place is terrible*, he thought, getting up and going to the counter. "Halloo. Could I have a large cheeseburger, chicken wings, large fries, and a Coke please!" he shouted, "Oh, and a strawberry ice cream with chocolate sprinkles on top," but still nobody answered.

"This is ridiculous," said Jefferson, "I suppose I will have to get it myself." He hopped over the counter to where all the food was laid out already cooked. He got a tray and loaded it up with two cheeseburgers, three bags of chicken wings, a very large bag of fries, a small, diet Coke (as he was watching his weight), and the biggest tub of strawberry ice cream with chocolate sprinkles that he could find, and sat back down.

He had just finished eating his ice cream when the door of the café opened, and in walked Bob along with Mr. Grimly, the owner of the zoo. "Jefferson!" shouted Mr. Grimly very crossly, shaking his finger at him. "You have been very, very bad. You have scared the life out of dozens of people at the zoo. You have caused goodness knows how many cars to crash along the road into town. You have terrorised a park full of children, completely trashed a home bakery, not to mention a ladies clothes shop. You burst an inflatable castle belonging to the leisure centre, nearly gave old Bob here a heart attack, and now where do I find you, sitting in a café, stuffing your face full of hamburgers, chicken wings, and ice cream. You, my lad, are in deep, deep trouble." Jefferson gulped.

"Sorry," he said, going bright red and looking very apologetic. "I only wanted to go for a walk, that's all. I didn't mean to harm anybody."

"Well," said Bob, quietly stroking Jefferson's neck, "I suppose there's no real harm done. But I think it's time to get back home. Don't you?"

Jefferson jumped down from his seat and took a last sip of his Coke. "Can I keep the hat?"

Mr. Grimly sighed, "All right, all right, if you must. But can we please get back to the zoo."

Jefferson grabbed his hat and smiled as Bob put a collar and a lead on him, and led him out of the leisure centre, into the back of a van. A few minutes later, he was back in his enclosure.

"Well," said his sister, running up to him excitedly. "Are you going to tell me what happened? And where on earth did you get that silly hat?"

Jefferson yawned, "Later," he said, "I will tell you later. First, I just want to have a doze."

Loki huffed off to roar at the monkeys while Jefferson lay down and closed his eyes. As he was drifting off to sleep, he smiled as he thought about all the adventures he had just had, and wondered what other new things would await him the next time he went to town.

The End

Rock Around the Waterhole

Gloria the hippo, loved singing, especially the latest pop songs. Every morning as soon as she got out of bed, she started. Firstly, she would do her breathing exercises. She would stand by the side of the waterhole and raise her arms high in the air as she breathed in, hold her breath for ten seconds, and then gently lower her arms as she breathed out. This she would do ten times, as regular as clockwork every morning. Then came her vocal exercises.

First there was a, "Mee Mee Mee Mee Mee Mee Meeee," quickly followed by a "Laa Laa Laa Laa Laa Laa Laaaa," and this would go on for half an hour or so until she felt sure that her vocal cords were in tip top condition.

Although Gloria loved her singing, it must be said that the rest of the inhabitants of the waterhole, especially the crocodiles, of whom there were four, didn't. "She's off again," groaned Marvin the oldest croc. "Oy Gloria, put a sock in it!" he shouted as Gloria began a rendition of "Circle of Life" from *The*

Lion King. "Don't you know what time it is? Some of us are still trying to sleep, and you sound like a two tonne alarm clock."

Gloria gave Marvin a look. "It is never too early for music, Marvin. Even you should know that." And she continued singing at the top of her voice, only this time it was her version of "Poker Face" by Lady GaGa. Marvin grunted and swam over to his mates who were scanning the banks of the waterhole for prey.

"This can't go on," he said, "there is only so much that a croc can take."

"Well, what can we do about it?" asked Rodger.

"I don't know," replied Marvin, "But we're gonna have to think of something before she drives me completely mad. Is it too much to ask to have a nice quiet waterhole, is it? Somewhere a croc can go about his business in peace. Catch the odd zebra, or just have a nice long wallow without having to listen to all that hullaballoo. Is that too much to hope for?"

"I know what you mean," added Bruce. "When was the last time you saw a wildebeest or something down here? And do you know why? Gloria has scared them all away with her singing. And what are we supposed to do? Starve!"

"I quite like her singing," said Walter sheepishly.

"Singing, you call that singing!" exclaimed Marvin. "It sounds more like a herd of elephants passing wind."

"She's not that bad," replied Walter. "I think she's really quite good."

"You would," retorted Rodger.

"And what's that supposed to mean?" asked Walter, getting slightly annoyed.

"You always were a bit of a wimp, Walter. Remember what happened the first time you saw a zebra in the water? You nearly jumped out of your scales and swam off screaming and crying like a big baby."

"That's not fair," replied Walter. "I was very young then and didn't know what it was."

"Rubbish. Even now you let us do all the hunting, and whinge and moan if we don't give you any," added Bruce.

"Yes, well, I'm just a bit nervous that's all," replied Walter.

"Are you all quite finished?" asked Marvin, looking at the others. "Can we get back to the problem in hand?"

"Sorry, Marvin," said Bruce. "So what are you going to do?"

"Why don't you go and have a word with her?" suggested Walter. "She's not a bad hippo and I'm sure she would listen to you, if you could try to be nice about it."

"Meaning what exactly?" asked Marvin.

"Well, you do have a tendency to be a bit, emm, grumpy shall we say," replied Walter.

"Me, grumpy? When have you ever seen me grumpy?"

"Quite often," replied Bruce.

"In fact, you're grumpy and bad tempered nearly all the time," added Rodger.

Marvin shrugged. "Yes, well you would be too if you had my teeth. Dr. Mbeki says he doesn't know how I keep going with my teeth. Says it's a wonder I'm able to eat at all. Did I ever tell you what he said?" The others groaned. Marvin was about to again relate the sordid and long history of his teeth, when he was nudged in the side by Bruce.

"Shhh, look over there." Marvin and the others looked to where Bruce was pointing. A lone wildebeest was making its way nervously down the bank towards the water, not fifty yards away.

"Breakfast," whispered Rodger excitedly.

"And dinner, and tea," added Marvin.

"I will stay here and keep lookout," said Walter, trying not to look embarrassed.

Marvin sighed, "Walter, you really are going to have to try and do a bit of hunting someday."

"I told you, I get too nervous," mumbled Walter.

"Forget about him and let's go," said Bruce. "What way do you want to do this?"

"You and Rodger approach from the sides, and I will attack head on," replied Marvin. Bruce and Rodger nodded and swam off towards their target that was now waist deep in the water. *This is going to be so easy*, thought Marvin as he swam just beneath the surface. Marvin halted about ten yards from the unsuspecting wildebeest. His body was completely submerged, except for his eyes. As he waited, he could see Bruce and Rodger getting into position. When he saw that they were ready, he gave the nod and all three crocodiles attacked. Marvin could taste the sweet fresh meat in his mouth as he opened his massive jaws.

Unfortunately however, it was at that precise moment that Gloria decided to let rip with the "Best of Both Worlds" from *Hannah Montana*. The wildebeest was so startled that it bolted out of water and ran up the bank to the safety of the plains. Marvin was furious as his jaws missed the wildebeest, and he was left with a mouthful of dirty water and mucky weeds.

"AAARGH, THAT'S IT," spluttered Marvin, "I HAVE HAD ENOUGH OF THAT STUPID HIPPO!" And he took off across the waterhole like a torpedo, with the others following close behind in his wake.

"What are you going to do?" asked Bruce, excitedly trying to keep up.

"Give that singing lump of lard a piece of my mind," snapped Marvin angrily.

"Please try and be nice about it," added Walter.

"Oh, shut up, Walter. I agree with Marvin; the time for being nice is over," growled Rodger.

"Oh dear. Well, if you're going to shout and lose your temper, I will just wait back here," said Walter.

"Whatever," replied Marvin as he reached the opposite bank, where Gloria had lapsed into a medley of songs by Michael Jackson, whilst trying to moonwalk. Marvin hauled himself out from the water on his short stubby legs, and shouted at Gloria. "GLORIA, ME AND THE BOYS HAVE HAD ENOUGH. YOU HAVE JUST RUINED THE ONLY CHANCE WE'VE HAD AT A DECENT MEAL IN WEEKS!"

Gloria stopped her singing and looked at Marvin. "Oh dear, Marvin, what's got you all in a tizzy? Teeth playing you up are they?" She then noticed the rest of the crocodiles and gave a little wave. "Hello boys." Rodger and Bruce ignored her, but Walter gave a little wave back.

"Hi Gloria, you're in fine voice this morning."

"Thank you, Walter. I find that it helps to sing in the morning before the air gets too warm and too dry."

"I never thought of that. I suppose it's easier on the old vocal cords."

"Walter!" shouted Marvin, "In case you have forgotten, we are not here to discuss the best time of the day to sing, but to put an end to the singing once and for all."

"Sorry," replied Walter, looking very embarrassed.

Marvin turned his attention back to Gloria. "No, my teeth are not playing me up, Gloria; it's you and your infernal singing that is playing me up. There's not a beast comes near this waterhole now because of the noise, and not only that but every time I close my eyes to have a bit of a doze, all that I can hear is you with your La La La's and your Da Da Da's. It's driving me crazy."

Gloria looked horrified, and took a sharp intake of breath. "I may La La Laa Marvin, but I have never, ever, Da Da Da-ed in my life," she protested.

"I don't care if you La La La, Da Da Da, or Sa Sa Sa," continued Marvin. "All I know is it has to stop. Either you quit the singing and give us all peace and quiet, or you can find yourself another waterhole. I mean it Gloria, that's the only two choices you have."

"You can't ask me to stop singing, Marvin. What else would I do?" answered Gloria, her voice trembling.

"I don't care what you do. Take up something quieter like knitting, or painting, or making model aeroplanes, or even stamp collecting, I really don't care," snapped Marvin. "But I will tell you one thing, if I hear so much as one single note ever again, then you are out of here."

"But what about my morning exercises?" protested Gloria.

"What about them? You'll not need them if you're not singing, will you?"

"But, but," continued Gloria.

"No buts Gloria. Either you stop the singing and let the waterhole have some peace and quiet, or you go. What's it to be?"

Gloria looked around the waterhole with huge tears running down her face. "But this is my home, I can't leave here."

"What you seem to have forgotten Gloria, is that this is our home as well. So what are you going to do?" Gloria thought for a moment and wiped the tears from her eyes.

"Okay, Marvin. If that is what you want, I will stop the singing," sobbed Gloria.

"Even the morning exercises?"

Gloria hesitated for a second then nodded. "Even the morning exercises," she added.

"Good. But remember, if I hear so much as one note . . ." added Marvin

"You won't, Marvin. I promise," replied Gloria, trying her best not to burst into floods of tears all over again.

Gloria watched as Marvin slid back into the water and joined his friends. She was absolutely heartbroken, so she took herself off to her bed, and cried until she could cry no more.

Over the next few weeks, the waterhole got back to normal. More and more animals came down to drink and the crocs hunted to their hearts content. In fact, they were so full that on some days they didn't need to hunt at all. Gloria, however, was totally and utterly miserable. She very rarely went into the water, preferring to sit on the bank singing softly in hushed, whispered tones to herself so that no one else, especially Marvin, could hear. She began to lose her appetite and went from a bubbly, happy-go-lucky hippo, to a big bag of misery. Everyone began to feel sorry for her, except for Marvin, who loved the peace and quiet.

"This is the life," he said to himself one morning after finishing off a large amount of zebra and having a doze, "plenty of grub, and not a sound to be heard." His sleep, however, was interrupted by Bruce and the others.

"Marvin, me and the boys want to talk to you," said Bruce.

"What about?" asked Marvin.

"Gloria," replied Walter.

"What about her?" asked Marvin.

"Look at her, Marvin," said Rodger, pointing at Gloria sitting on the opposite bank. "She's miserable and it's our fault."

"We want you to tell her she can sing again," said Bruce.

Marvin was gobsmacked. "Please tell me you are joking," he replied.

"No we're not, Marvin. We all miss her singing.

Don't we boys?" added Rodger. Bruce and Walter nodded.

"But we agreed," protested Marvin.

"I know, I know," said Bruce, "but I never thought it would make her this unhappy."

"Maybe we could reach some sort of agreement," suggested Walter. "Let her sing at the weekends or something."

"I don't believe you three," sighed Marvin. "She and her singing were making our lives miserable."

"That doesn't mean we should make hers miserable," said Bruce.

Marvin looked at each of his friends. "Is that what you all want?"

"Yes," replied Rodger.

Marvin sighed. "Right, okay. If that's what you want I will go and talk to her. But only at weekends, clear?"

"Clear," replied the others.

"I can't believe I'm doing this," said Marvin to himself as he swam over to where Gloria was sitting.

Gloria saw Marvin approach and got to her feet. "I wasn't singing, Marvin, honestly I wasn't." Marvin pushed himself out of the water and onto the bank.

"It's okay, Gloria. That's what I have come to talk to you about. Me and the boys were thinking. Although we love the peace and quiet, maybe we, or should I say I, have been a bit harsh. I really didn't mean to make you so unhappy, so if you want you can sing on Fridays, Saturdays, and Sundays, and do your morning exercises again."

Gloria burst into tears of joy, and ran down the bank lifting Marvin in her arms and hugging him as hard as she could. "Thank you, Marvin, thank you. You don't know how happy that has made me, and I was thinking that if you like, I could maybe give a little concert for everyone on Sunday afternoons. You and the boys could join me as my backing group. You could call yourselves "Rock Around the Croc" what do you think?"

"That's a brilliant idea," said Walter, who had followed Bruce and Rodger up onto the bank behind Marvin. "We could rehearse on Friday and Saturday, and then give the concert on Sunday. What about it Marvin, are you in?"

"Me," answered Marvin hesitantly, "I'm afraid I'm not much of a singer."

"Don't be silly," laughed Gloria. "I'll soon whip you into shape. It would be so much fun. I mean, what else is there to do around here at the weekend?" Marvin looked at Gloria's beaming face and then at his friends.

"Well, I suppose if you can't beat them, you might as well join them," he sighed. "But only at weekends Gloria, and you stop singing during the week after your morning exercises, promise?"

Gloria was beside herself with joy. "I promise, Marvin. Now, let's see; today is Wednesday, so in two days time we can start to practice and have our first concert this weekend. Oh, this is going to be so much fun! Walter, what songs do you know?"

Gloria walked off with Walter, Bruce, and Rodger talking excitedly and suggesting songs for their first concert, leaving Marvin alone on the bank. Marvin smiled to himself. It was nice to see Gloria happy again and in a funny way, this probably was the norm for the waterhole, not the peace and quiet of the past few weeks, no matter how much he enjoyed it. He then suddenly had an idea and ran after the others. "Hold on, wait for me," he shouted, "I've just remembered, I know some *High School Musical* numbers I could do."

The End

When Bradley Got Left Behind

Hannah was in her room unpacking her suitcase and putting things away when she suddenly shouted, "Dad dad, Bradley's not here!" Her dad was downstairs getting things out of the car and shouted back up to her.

"What's wrong, Hannah?"

"It's Bradley; he's not here. We must have left him behind," cried Hannah.

"When did you last see him?" asked her dad, coming up the stairs.

"He was sitting on the top bunk whenever we were packing up the car. I must have forgot to lift him. What are we going to do?" Hannah started to cry, but her dad put his arm around her to comfort her.

"There, there," he said. "Don't worry; we will ring the hotel and see if anyone has found him."

Bradley was Hannah's favourite bear. She got him a couple of years before on holidays in Scotland, and he went everywhere with her. He was brown with a cream-coloured face and he wore a red baseball cap, a yellow shirt with blue flowers on it, blue shorts, and red boots. Hannah adored Bradley and every night when she went to bed, she always made sure that she had Bradley tucked up under her arm.

That weekend Hannah, her mum, dad, and her little sister Katie, had stayed at a posh hotel down by the seaside. Bradley knew that he would be going as well, and was very excited. When the morning came that they were to leave, Bradley could hardly wait. He jumped off Hannah's bed, climbed up onto the radiator below Hannah's bedroom window, and watched as her dad loaded the suitcases into the car.

"Yippee!" he shouted. "We will be leaving soon. I better get back on the bed so Hannah doesn't forget me." So he climbed back down, lay on the bed, and waited patiently for Hannah. A few minutes later, Hannah came bouncing into the room.

"Come on, Bradley," she said, "time to get into the car." So she took Bradley outside and sat him on

her knee as her dad strapped her into her car seat. As they drove along, Hannah told Bradley about all the wonderful, fun things that they were going to do over the weekend. "We'll go to the beach and the pool in the hotel and do lots of things," she said, "and you will sleep beside me in a bunk bed on the top bunk; won't that be fun?" Bradley couldn't wait.

At last they arrived at the hotel. Hannah's dad spoke to the lady at the front desk, and then they went down to their room. It was just as Hannah said. There were bunk beds, and Hannah climbed up to the top one. "This is where we are going to sleep," she said to Bradley, "so I will have to hold onto you extra tight to make sure you don't roll over and fall out." Her mum and dad had a big bed, and there was a little cot for Katie.

After they got settled in and put their clothes away, they all went to the pool before having their tea. Hannah and Katie loved splashing in the warm water, while Bradley sat at the side and watched as everyone enjoyed themselves. He didn't mind that he wasn't able to go into the water as well, as long as Hannah had a good time, that's all that mattered.

After their swim, they went back to their room and got ready for their tea. They all went into the restaurant and sat at a very posh table. Hannah sat beside her dad, and Katie was in a high chair beside her mum. Bradley meanwhile sat in a chair of his very own beside Hannah, and felt very important. When the food came it looked delicious! Dad had a steak, Mum had chicken, Katie had chicken—all blended down with potatoes, vegetables, and gravy, as she can't chew very well—and Hannah had chicken dinosaurs with fries and peas. Then after that, they all had chocolate cake and ice cream. *Hmm, that looks delicious*, thought Bradley to himself.

When they had finished eating their meal, they went for a walk around the grounds of the hotel. At the back of the hotel behind some trees, was an adventure playground for the children. Hannah put Bradley down the slide, which was his favourite thing. Then he went on the swings and the roundabout, which made him feel a bit dizzy. Very soon it was getting dark and time for bed.

After Hannah got washed and cleaned her teeth, she put on her pyjamas and climbed up into bed where Bradley was already waiting for her. She propped Bradley up on her pillows and read some stories to him from a book that she brought with her from home. In no time at all, Hannah was fast asleep, with her arms wrapped tightly around Bradley as usual.

The next morning after breakfast, they all went to the beach. It was a lovely sunny day and the sand was nice and warm on Hannah's toes. Mum had brought a picnic with her, and Dad put some big towels and rugs on the sand for them to sit on. Dad took Katie down to the sea for a paddle, whilst Mummy read a magazine. Hannah got her net and bucket and went exploring in the rock pools to see if she could catch anything, and of course, Bradley went with her.

While Hannah searched in the pools of sea water, Bradley sat on the rocks feeling slightly nervous in case he fell in, but Hannah always made sure that he was perfectly safe. After they had their picnic, they went for a walk into town to the Funfair. Inside there were loads of different rides to go on, which were all covered in brightly coloured lights that twinkled, glittered, and danced around the amusement arcade.

Hannah and her dad went on the dodgem cars, with Bradley sitting on Hannah's knee. Bradley thought it was great fun right up until the first time that another car bumped into them. Hannah screamed and shrieked with laughter and delight, as her dad drove around trying to avoid other people who were trying to crash into them. Bradley, however, didn't like it one little bit, and couldn't wait for the ride to stop so that he could get off.

After the dodgems, Hannah and Bradley went on the Helter Skelter, the Carousel, the Ghost Train, and then on to the park. At the park, they all went on a boat shaped like a swan, and paddled around the boating lake. When they had finished at the park, they went to a café for ice cream, and in no time at all it was time to head back to the hotel for their tea. After tea, they went back to their room to pack. Mum said that she would stay and start to pack up some things as they were leaving the next morning, so Dad took Hannah and Bradley for one last swim in the pool.

Bradley felt sad that the holiday was nearly over, but he also missed being back in Hannah's bedroom along with all his friends. There was Nessie the Loch Ness monster, William the brown teddy bear, Cat in the Hat, Tinkerbelle the fairy from *Peter Pan*, and Sponge Bob Square Pants, who Bradley thought was a bit rude at times, but liked anyway as he could also be really funny and make them all laugh.

The morning that they were to go home was really, really busy. After breakfast, Hannah, Katie, and Bradley sat watching television, while Mum and Dad got everything ready to go home. When everything was packed, Dad asked Hannah to bring her suitcase out to the car, so she left Bradley on the top bunk. Soon, the car was packed up and they were all ready to leave. Dad handed the keys back to the lady at the desk, got Hannah and Katie into their seats, and an hour later they were home. That was when Hannah realized what had happened.

"What are we going to do, Dad? Can we drive back to the hotel and get Bradley?"

"Let's just ring first and make sure he is there. Are you sure you have looked in all the suitcases?"

"Yes," cried Hannah, the tears rolling down her cheeks.

"Don't worry," said her dad, "We'll get him back." And off her dad went to telephone the hotel.

Meanwhile, back at the hotel, Bradley was sitting up on the bunk bed looking around and wondering where on earth Hannah had got to. Suddenly, the door opened. *About time*, thought Bradley, *I was starting to think that Hannah had forgotten about me.* But it wasn't Hannah; it was the cleaning lady who had come to clean the room and change the sheets on the bed.

"My goodness," said the lady, lifting Bradley up. "What have we got here then? Looks like someone has left you behind," she continued as she put Bradley on her trolley. Bradley felt really miserable. Hannah had left him behind. Now he would never see her or his friends ever again. How could she do this? How could she leave her best friend lying on the bed and go home without him? If the cleaning lady had looked really closely, she would have seen tiny tears starting to roll down Bradley's face, getting his fur all wet.

After the cleaning lady had finished in the room, she took Bradley up to the reception desk and handed him over to the receptionist. "Found this little chap in room 22," she said. "It would appear that he has been left behind."

"Not to worry," said the receptionist, kindly, "I will look after him." Bradley was taken to a storeroom, and put on a shelf along with other toys that must have been left in the hotel by their owners. There were teddies, dolls, robots, balls, games, and dozens and dozens of buckets and spades. As they lady closed the door behind her, the room became very dark, making Bradley feel very scared, and very, very lonely.

"Left behind were you?" asked a very large, brown bear that was sitting next to him.

Bradley nodded, "It was an accident. Hannah will come back for me," he sobbed. The big bear laughed.

"Do you think so? That's what I thought when they put me in here, and I'm still here."

"How long have you been here?" asked Bradley, drying the tears from his eyes.

93

"Nearly a year," replied the bear. "Believe me; no one is coming back for you. Your little Hannah will get another bear to take your place."

"Leave him alone, Growler," said a very pretty doll in a red and yellow dress. "Maybe he will be lucky and his owner will come back for him." She then smiled at Bradley. "What's your name?" she asked softly.

"Bradley," replied Bradley, trying his best to be brave.

"Well Bradley," said the doll, "take no notice of old Growler there. He's always in a bad mood. You shift over and come and sit beside me." Bradley shuffled along the shelf until he was sitting beside the doll.

"What's your name?" asked Bradley.

"Annabelle," said the doll, "and I am pleased to meet you Bradley," she continued.

"How long have you been here?" asked Bradley, looking round at all the rest of the toys.

"Not long," replied Annabelle, "just a couple of weeks. But I know that the little girl who owns me, Molly, is coming to collect me in a few days time. So in the meantime, I will just have to be patient and wait."

"Hah!" laughed Growler. "That's what you said last week."

"Well, maybe she was busy last week!" shouted Annabelle.

"Rubbish," snapped Growler. "You just can't accept the fact that you have been forgotten about just like the rest of us, and that the same thing will happen to your friend there."

"My Molly WILL come back for me," said Annabelle angrily. "But your owner was probably glad to see the back of you. You are so bad tempered and grumpy; that is why you are still sitting here all this time."

"We'll see. We'll see," said Growler.

Bradley sat on the shelf in the dark, and put his little paws up to his face. "Please Hannah," he whispered to himself, "please don't leave me here. Please come back for me." And he lay down on the shelf, closed his eyes, and cried himself to sleep.

The next morning the door of the storeroom opened and the receptionist lady came in. All the toys were looking at her excitedly, hoping that it was their owner who had come back for them. Annabelle was the most excited of the all. "Molly, it's my molly. She's come back for me. I just know it is," she whispered to Bradley. She sat up, smoothed the creases out of her dress, and put on her best smile. The lady reached up her hand towards Annabelle, but instead of lifting her, she lifted Bradley.

"Come on," she said, "there is a little girl in reception bursting to see you."

Bradley saw the disappointment of Annabelle's face. "Maybe next time," he whispered to her as he was taken out of the room. Annabelle smiled and nodded her head.

"Bye Bradley," she said quietly, and waving slightly. "It was lovely to meet you and I am glad your owner came back."

As Bradley watched, the lady switched off the light of the storeroom and Annabelle, still waving and smiling, along with the rest of the toys faded into the darkness. Although Bradley was glad that Hannah had come back for him, he also felt sad for all the toys left behind, with no boys or girls to play with. His sadness suddenly disappeared, however, as he heard Hannah shouting his name.

"Bradley! Bradley! I am so sorry. I didn't mean to leave you here. Please forgive me." Bradley was back in Hannah's arms, and he was overjoyed. Her dad had driven back up to the hotel to collect him, after he had discovered that the cleaning lady had found him in the room, and now he was back where he belonged.

As her dad got Hannah into the car, she took Bradley in her arms and kissed his cheeks. "Know what?" said Hannah, as she hugged her bear. "No matter where we go or what we do, I am going to make you a promise that never, ever again will you be left behind." As Bradley sat on Hannah's knee, her dad started up the car, and drove out of the hotel car park to take Hannah, and more importantly Bradley, back home.

The End

LaVergne, TN USA
23 March 2011
221283LV00003B